A Bride For

Jacob

Book Three
Brides of Broken Arrow

Cheryl Wright

Cheryl Wright

A BRIDE FOR JACOB
Book Three
Brides of Broken Arrow

Copyright ©2021 by Cheryl Wright

Cover Artist: Black Widow Books

Editing: Amber Downey

Dedication

To Margaret Tanner, my very dear friend and fellow author, for her enduring encouragement and friendship.

To Alan, my husband of over forty-six years, who has been a relentless supporter of my writing and dreams for many years.

To Virginia McKevitt, my cover artist and friend, who always creates the most amazing covers for my books, thank you.

To You, my wonderful readers, who encourage me to continue writing these stories. It is such a joy knowing so many of you enjoy reading my stories as much as I love writing them for you.

Cheryl Wright

Table of Contents

Chapter One

Helena, Montana – 1880's

Clarissa Reyes sat amongst her siblings and fumed. Every last one of them harassed her for being a spinster.

Her three younger sisters had been married off long ago, whether they'd agreed or not. Being her stubborn self, Clarissa had refused to marry under duress, and stormed out when potential suitors came to visit. Her parents and five brothers did not approve. Her sisters admired her courage, even if they only did so privately. She knew what she wanted, and it wasn't to marry some stuffy admirer who came to court her.

It was her choice who she married, and she'd told her family so, to her detriment. Gentleman callers gave up, the type Father thought worthy anyway. But wasn't that exactly what she wanted? A year ago, Clarissa would have agreed, but now she felt like the odd one out. Apart from the fact she found herself feeling lonely a lot of the time. All her friends were long married, and with no chaperone, she was forbidden to visit anywhere and was therefore stuck in the house.

Her five brothers were scattered about the room, and each one studied her. With both their parents dead after a horrific accident just days earlier, they had begun to pressure her again, especially Henry, who was the eldest. Oh, she knew why – nothing got past Clarissa. Henry wanted to sell the house and pocket the proceeds. To do that, he had to marry her off and get her out of the house.

The last of the mourners had left the family home less than thirty minutes earlier. Couldn't they have at least waited until Mother and Father were cold? They'd be rolling in their freshly dug graves right now, she was certain of it.

Mother understood her; she always said Clarissa was a free spirit, but all that did was rile her father. He'd stormed off on more than one occasion and demanded Mother find a suitable husband for her immediately.

Tears filled her eyes at the thought of never seeing her parents again.

"What about Jefferson Dimple," Henry asked.

Her heart sank. The last thing she needed was to be married off to that fool. If she was being forced into marriage, surely her brothers could find someone more suitable? Clarissa sunk further down into her chair.

"Or Hank Mulberry." It was James this time. He finished the sentence with a chuckle. Everyone knew about Hank. He was the town imbecile and far worse than Jefferson Dimple, although he did have money, his one and only redeeming feature.

Clarissa forced back her tears. If she didn't do something, and do it quick, she would be in a bucketload of trouble. She'd be married to some buffoon, albeit a rich buffoon, and there would be no chance of happiness. It was the one thing she'd told her mother she craved.

Theodore Black, or Teddy as most people knew him, sat behind his impressive desk. He had been the Reyes family lawyer for as long as Clarissa could remember.

"Clarissa," Teddy said in surprise as he stood. "I am sorry about your parents. They were very special people."

"Thank you," she said quietly. *Was she even going to go through with this?* "I, I need your help." As soon as the words were out, she wasn't even certain Teddy would be able to help with this problem.

She studied the much older man as he stared at her, then raised his eyebrows. "If it's about your inheritance…"

"As the oldest son, Henry gets everything. I know that. This is different. I need…" She almost couldn't bring herself to say the words, but knew she had to. "I need to get married, and quickly. Henry is trying his darndest to marry me off to whatever fool he can convince to do so." She scowled. "I'm sure he's offering a dowry, or maybe a reward, for someone to take me off his hands." She reached for the chair and quickly sat. *How much was a person meant to endure?*

Teddy studied her. "Why would Henry do such a thing? Your brother is an upstanding man, like your entire family." He appeared quite perplexed.

"The sale of the family home will fetch a pretty penny. I'm certain it has nothing to do with my happiness, and everything to do with how much Henry will earn from the sale." Her chin quivered, and Clarissa turned away from his gaze.

"Would you like some water?" he asked out of the blue, but didn't wait for an answer. Clarissa understood it was Teddy's way of not having to deal with a blubbering female. Leaving the room for long enough to allow her to compose herself would solve the problem. He returned a few minutes later with a large tumbler of water and handed it to her.

Teddy put a hand to her shoulder, then sat down behind his desk again. "How quickly do you need to marry?"

"It's urgent," she said, glancing over the rim of the glass. "If I wait more than a day or two, it will be too late.

Teddy considered her carefully, then shuffled some papers around. "As it happens, I may be able to assist. There's a young man in Halliwell who is looking for a wife. He is not as wealthy as your father, but he has substantial wealth, and comes from a good family. I've known them for many years, at least as long as your own family."

Clarissa's heart pounded. She didn't care about money. As she'd told her mother many times, happiness was her only concern. Still, having a husband to support her in the manner she was used to would be quite pleasing.

She straightened her shoulders and sat taller in the chair. "Please arrange it, Teddy. As I mentioned earlier, I believe it's crucial for me to marry in the next two days at most." She stood and turned to leave, her head pounding at what she'd just done. Never did she believe she would be marrying a man she didn't know or had no inkling about. She didn't even know his name. She forced herself to stay upright as lightheadedness began to overtake her.

"I'll be in touch very soon," he said quietly, and Clarissa left his office.

She breathed in the fresh air as she left the confines of Teddy's office. What had she done? Her life would be forever changed, but she knew if she'd not taken this drastic step, Henry would make arrangements on her behalf, and Clarissa's life would be a misery forever more.

The moment she returned home, she would begin packing for her long journey to her new life. As the family buggy took her back home, she had a sudden thought. What if this so far nameless young man decided not to marry her? What would she do *then*? The thought left her feeling hollow.

Chapter Two

Clarissa paid the driver, then stood outside her new home, luggage at her feet.

She stared at the building for long moments. It might have been imposing compared to the cottages she saw on the property on the way in, but compared to her family home, it was small. Her family had been, and still were pillars of society. She knew little about Jacob Adams and his family except what Teddy had told her.

Jacob was the oldest and the last of the three brothers to marry, but in his case, there was no necessity to marry under the conditions of his father's will. But also, according to Teddy, Noah and Seth had been forced to marry to meet the conditions and keep their respective properties. Her situation wasn't rosy, but at least her father hadn't imposed such dreadful constraints on her. Not that it would have surprised Clarissa if he had done so; he desperately wanted to see his eldest daughter finally married.

Well, now his wish had come to fruition, but he wasn't around to see it happen.

Clarissa adjusted the stylish hat sitting on her head, and straightened her ruffled gown. Her luggage was far too heavy for her to lift, so she would leave it to her husband's servants to carry inside. She licked her suddenly dry lips, rolled her stiff shoulders, and ambled toward the door. She wasn't due for some days yet, but the moment she told Henry she had secretly married, he insisted she leave immediately. She was surprised he hadn't objected to Clarissa taking her possessions, and wouldn't have been surprised in the least if he'd confiscated them. After all, money seemed to be more important to him than his sister.

Her heart was heavy from the events of the recent past, but she vowed to begin a new and better life with her husband. Teddy assured her that marrying by proxy was the best way, because then she couldn't be rushed into marriage with someone else. He was right – Henry had wanted to marry her off to Jefferson Dimple that very day. Oh, he was rich, she'd give him that, but a gentleman he was not.

She lifted her hand and knocked on the door. A shiver went down her spine; *what was Jacob Adams like?* Teddy had told her very little. The door slowly opened, and her heart fluttered.

"Hello? Can I help you?" *Was this woman his mother?* Clarissa brushed the thought away; she was surely far too young to be his mother.

"Mrs. Adams? I'm looking for Mr. Adams. Er, Jacob."

The woman who appeared to be in her late thirties raised her eyebrows. "Mrs. Adams died long ago, my dear. I'm Miss Laura Massey, Jacob's housekeeper."

"I humbly apologize," she said quietly, as she felt the heat crawl up her neck and face at her blunder. She had no idea her husband's mother was dead. "I'm Clarissa Reyes…er, Adams."

The woman's face broke into a grin. "Oh my! We weren't expecting you yet. Jacob," she called over her shoulder. "Come in, come in," she said, opening the door wider. "Oh, this is so exciting. My little Jacob has a wife."

It was Clarissa's turn to raise her eyebrows. Just how short was her husband for the housekeeper to call him little?

She glanced up as a figure appeared in the hallway. "You called, Miss Massey?" He began to stroll toward them, then paused as he saw Clarissa standing there. *Had he guessed who she was?* A shiver went down her spine as he studied her. No photographs were exchanged – there hadn't been time. In fact, they knew little about each other, which had been another reason for Clarissa's nerves. Teddy had assured her Jacob was a good man, and given her unpleasant situation, she had to take his word for it.

"Hello," he said as he got closer. "Do I know you?" Then as though everything fell into place, his whole demeanor changed, and his face broke into a grin. "Clarissa?" He reached out a hand and shook hers. She stared down at their entwined hands. *Would he always shake her hand? She certainly hoped not.* "Welcome. I wasn't expecting you until next week."

She nodded. "My eldest brother made my situation at home untenable, so I left earlier than planned. My luggage is outside," she said, looking over her shoulder as though he had no idea where to find it. It made her feel like an utter fool. "I'm sorry. That was a stupid thing to say."

He stood grinning down at her. Why on earth she had expected Jacob to be short in stature she had no idea. Oh, yes she did. Miss Massey had called him *little Jacob*. She turned to the woman. "Why did you call him little Jacob? My husband must be at least six foot tall."

The housekeeper laughed. "He was little when I came here to care for him after his mother died."

Jacob turned red with embarrassment. "That was a long time ago, Miss Massey. I'm not your little boy anymore," he said quietly.

He went outside and snatched up the luggage. "Take it straight to your bedroom," Miss Massey instructed. Jacob did as he was told. "Now go outside. Both of you," she demanded when he returned.

Clarissa was confused, and Jacob appeared perplexed as well. The older woman stood grinning at the pair. "Now carry your bride over the threshold." She raised her eyebrows, then turned away and left them alone.

Jacob grinned, then picked Clarissa up off the ground as though she was weightless. "I don't mind if I do." He stared down into her face. "You are quite beautiful," he said breathlessly after studying her, and a shiver of delight went down her spine. He stared into her face for what seemed an endless amount of time, then began to step toward the door. After carrying her over the threshold he stood in the parlor, still staring at her. It was as though he didn't know what to do next.

"You can put me down now," she said quietly, although truth be told, Clarissa was enjoying being held by her new husband. He was quite handsome, and she could gaze into his striking blue eyes for a lifetime. Hopefully, that's exactly what she would do.

"This is the master bedroom," he said, glancing about. "There should be plenty of room for your clothes in here," he said opening the door to a large wardrobe. He stood the traveling trunk upright and unfastened the multiple leather straps then opened it for his wife. Her father had spared no expense purchasing this lavish trunk for his daughter. If she recalled correctly, it was for her first ever river cruise. Even at fifteen, she'd thought it rather opulent, but Father would have none of it. Even back then he'd spared no expense for her gowns. She was a member of the renowned Reyes family and had to look the part he'd told her on several occasions. "Once you've unpacked, I'll give you a tour of the place." She stared up at him. She'd been lost in her thoughts; had he noticed?

Jacob gazed down into the trunk. He studied the interior with its floral lining, five deep drawers on one side, and hanging space on the other. "You have a lot of clothes." He finally said, as his brows furrowed.

"When you are the daughter of an influential man such as my father, you must look the part."

"You sound as though you've recited that line many times before."

It had been drummed into her since she was old enough to understand. Being the eldest daughter made it far worse for her than her sisters who were much younger than Clarissa. "If you only knew," she said quietly, then began to remove her clothing from the trunk and store it away.

"I emptied these drawers for you too," Jacob said. "For your, er, delicates or whatever you want to use them for." His cheeks flushed bright red, which Clarissa thought rather endearing.

"Thank you." She delved into the trunk again, and he left her alone. She glanced about the room. It was rather beautiful, but not as big as her own bedroom back home. This room was pleasantly decorated, but it was obvious the décor had not been updated for sometime. Perhaps since his mother had passed on.

There were several items of furniture, but the one that stood out the most was the bed. The bed she and Jacob would share tonight. Clarissa swallowed down the thought. She had literally met her husband minutes ago, but was expected to share his bed in a matter of hours, and no doubt have relations with him. The thought terrified her.

Jacob ducked his head around the bedroom door. "Have you finished your unpacking?" He'd tried to give her time and space, but had become frustrated after thirty minutes. Surely it didn't take that long to empty one trunk, albeit a large one? His bride did have a lot of luggage, but still…

She spun around to stare at him. "I, I wasn't sure where to put my toiletries. You may remove the trunk now though."

He glanced across at the polished dressing table sitting to one side of the room. The same one she'd presumably added her undergarments too – he'd bought it especially for her, since his housekeeper had suggested his wife would need something along those lines. It was beautifully made, and he'd picked it out especially for her. There were four drawers either side, and another two delicate draws on top at the back. Nestled in between them was a large mirror. The ornate etchings set it apart from all the other furniture in the room which had belonged to his parents. "You may use the dresser. It's yours to do as you please." *Why hadn't he thought to tell her that earlier?* He'd placed the matching satinwood chair in front of the dresser for her exclusive use. He hoped the pastel blue of the padded seat would be pleasing to his wife.

Jacob felt incredibly nervous. He wasn't what you'd call uncomfortable around his wife, but a little uneasy was probably a better description. He hoped that would change in the days to come. "Miss Massey has made tea when you are ready, but I thought we might do a quick tour first?"

She stared at him momentarily and seemed to look down her nose at him. Teddy mentioned she'd come from a high profile family in Helena, but he apparently hadn't told him enough. Did Clarissa think she was too good for him? Well, it was far too late if she did; they were married and there was nothing either of them could do about it now. "What business was your father in?" he abruptly asked, trying to get some insight into his wife's background. She turned to face him and winced. He immediately wished he could take the words back. After all, what did it matter?

"He was," she swallowed back her emotions. "the banker, and owned half of Helena."

Her eyes glistened with unshed tears and Jacob felt deep regret at his question. He stepped toward her and put his arms around his distressed wife. "I'm sorry. I didn't mean to pry, or to upset you," he said gently.

She immediately stiffened in his arms. "I am perfectly fine," she said, conviction in her voice. He had no doubt she'd been brought up to never show her emotions. He hoped that would change over time.

She suddenly stepped out of his embrace. "Shall we begin the tour?" Her chin went up, and she stood aside and waited for Jacob to lead.

As they worked their way through the house, Jacob had the distinct feeling Clarissa was unimpressed with her new home. It was the largest property in the entire region, and their home was far bigger than the cottages his brothers had chosen to build for their families. He felt a wall building between them and had no idea how to tear it down.

Clarissa sat opposite her husband in the parlor and sipped her tea. She was almost certain the best china had been produced on her behalf and was sure they would normally drink from mugs. Teddy had assured her she was marrying a decent man from a wealthy family. She wouldn't have agreed otherwise.

Under normal circumstances her brothers would have checked him out and ensured he was of good standing and worthy of her hand in marriage. Unfortunately, that was out of the question in this case, and she'd had to take her chances. Jacob seemed nice enough, and she was certain he was wealthy since Teddy said it was the case, but he didn't appear to be in the same league as her father. Then again, who was? Father had made a move to takeover the railway when the accident happened;

her brother Henry vowed to follow through on the offer. Clarissa was certain he would, particularly when it would mean far more income for the family in the long run. Not that she would see even one cent of that money. She had essentially been left a pauper. If it hadn't been for the allowance Mother insisted on, she wouldn't have had money to even get to her husband. Teddy had offered money for expenses, but she refused; she was far too proud for that.

"This is lovely. Thank you, Miss Massey," she said after swallowing down a mouthful of the dainty cupcake made the housekeeper

"Oh my Lord! Can we start off with you calling me Laura? I've tried for years to get Jacob to stop calling me Miss all the time." The housekeeper rolled her eyes.

Clarissa couldn't help herself, she chuckled. "You remind me of Daisy, my personal maid back home." She immediately stopped talking. Both Laura and her husband appeared shocked at her words. Too late she realized what a privileged life she had led compared to most.

Laura suddenly composed herself. "Was she also a friend?" Her words were gentle, controlled.

"She was."

"Then you shall miss her. I hope one day we too, will become friends." Laura lifted her cup and began to drink her tea again.

Clarissa stared out the window at the vast expanse of land. Her husband was kind and wealthy, but most importantly, she was safe, despite everything being totally different to what she'd expected. Her life had completely changed since the death of her dear parents, and her brothers couldn't wait to be rid of her so they could sell the house and pocket the proceeds. The question was, would she adjust to this new life? And would she eventually come to care for her husband or would she only tolerate him because she had no choice in the matter? Only time would tell.

Chapter Three

Clarissa hovered in the doorway to the master bedroom. She had dreaded this moment all day. A determined spinster, her mother had never given her *the talk*. The one where secrets were passed from mother to daughter about what transpired between husband and wife. As a result, she was totally oblivious to what she should expect in her marital bed.

Jacob sat on the side of the bed, the bed she would share with him from now on, unbuttoning his shirt. He glanced up and smiled, apparently trying to put her at ease. It wasn't working. Just seeing him there half undressed set her heart to racing – surely that was due to not knowing what the future held? What the next minutes held?

He must have sensed her discomfort because he stood, his arm outreached, motioning for her to enter the room. She was frozen to the spot and couldn't make her legs work. Her brain was not connecting either, and she stood there feeling like an utter fool. "It's all right, Clarissa," Jacob said gently, then stepped toward her, his hand coaxing her. When he finally reached the spot where she stood, his arm snaked tenderly around her waist and he guided her into the room. "There's nothing to be afraid of, I promise."

She glanced up into his face. It was devoid of all emotion and she wondered what he was thinking. *That his wife was afraid of him?* It wasn't far from the truth, but she wasn't fearful of Jacob. She was worried of what would occur once they were alone in that bed. Her eyes roamed over the beautifully carved canopy bed that had served his parents for many years. She opened her mouth to speak, but the words didn't come. Instead, she nodded her head, then glanced up into his face.

Jacob had made her feel at home from the moment she'd arrived. He'd been kind and accommodating, and she had no reason to fear him. He pulled her close. "You're shaking," he said, and enveloped her in his strong but tender arms. "Don't be afraid. I promise not to hurt you. Ever." His head came down and his lips covered hers, ever so gentle at first, but then more passionately. She'd read about passionate kisses in novels, but Jacob's kiss was far better than anything she could have imagined. Soon he was removing her clothing, slowly and bit by little bit, and it set her heart to racing all over again. When she stood naked in the middle of the room, he picked her up and set her down on the bed. Their bed. Clarissa soon became Jacob's wife in every sense of the word, and she wasn't complaining.

Clarissa woke the next morning in a tangle of sheets as well as her husband's arms and legs. It was as though she was living in a dream and not reality. A mere two weeks ago she was out on the town with her mother arranging outfits for an upcoming ball. Not that Clarissa was interested in looking for a husband, which was Mother's objective. Clarissa's intention was to attend the ball and have a good time. For the last several years she'd attended at Mother's insistence, and not once did she feel even a sliver of excitement dancing with the variety of young gentlemen in attendance. No, it was merely a social event where she could mingle and enjoy herself.

The memory was bittersweet. She'd enjoyed her time with her mother that day; the measuring up for her ball gown, the buggy ride into town, and also the luncheon they'd taken at *Aunty Shelley's* exclusive diner. *Aunt Shelley's* was booked up for months ahead. It so happened Mother had booked four dates in advance – one for each of her daughters. Anna Reyes had a permanent booking this time every year. She wanted to spend time with her daughters more than anything in the world. As it transpired, Clarissa's *date* with her mother was only days before Anna's untimely death.

Little did either of them know it would be their last full day together. Tears shimmered in her eyes at the thought, and Clarissa swallowed down her emotion. The last thing she wanted was to become a blubbering wreck in front of her new husband.

"Good morning," he said quietly as he caressed her cheek. Clarissa turned to face him, and he captured her lips with his own. "How are you feeling this morning?"

How was she feeling? Like she'd fallen off a horse and been dragged along by the stirrup. Not that she would admit that to her handsome husband. "I'm fine. What about you?" She stared into his blue eyes and was almost lost in them.

"I'm the best I've been for a very long time. And to think I was nervous about marrying you, sight unseen." He continued to caress her cheek.

Her heart pounded. That was exactly the way Clarissa had felt, but Teddy had reassured her Jacob was a good person, a kind person, and she had nothing to worry about. So far that appeared to be true. "I suppose we'd better get out of bed." He stared directly into her face. "Unless there's some reason for us to linger." He wiggled his eyebrows and smiled. Clarissa couldn't resist him, didn't really want to resist him, and Jacob soon dragged her in under the bedding. At this rate she would need a hot bath to work out all the aches and pains of the muscles she wasn't used to using.

"Good morning to you both," Laura said as she hovered over the woodfired stove. "You're late rising today, Jacob." She raised her eyebrows just a touch and Clarissa felt one foot tall. Laura had obviously guessed what they'd been doing, and Clarissa was certain her cheeks were beet red with embarrassment. As though he sensed her discomfort, Jacob pulled her close to him and leaned in to kiss her forehead.

"I thought I'd give you a tour of the ranch today. If you're up to it, that is." He glanced down at her for mere seconds. "You must be exhausted after all the travel you did to get here."

"It was rather tiring, but I did stay overnight in a hotel, so that helped a little."

He reached for her hands and held them in front of himself. "I'm glad. I hate the thought of you traveling alone."

His words sent a shiver down her spine. He *was* the caring man Teddy had said he was. "It would have been terribly worrying if we hadn't already been married. A single woman traveling alone can be quite dangerous."

Now he frowned. "I'm sorry. I really wasn't thinking." He pulled her close and hugged her tight. "Was it frightening? I certainly hope not."

She pushed herself away and glanced up at him. "It was at first, especially combined with the fact I had fled the house without telling anyone. If something happened, no one would have even known. Thankfully, once we were on the move and I was settled, I felt perfectly safe."

"Good."

"If you two have finished with the small talk, your breakfast is ready." Laura held a plate loaded with steaming pancakes and motioned for them to move into the dining room. "Although it's closer to lunch time than breakfast," she said under her breath.

Clarissa felt the heat rise up from her neck again. Jacob apparently thought it funny since he laughed out loud. Despite having five brothers, she would never understand men.

"This is delicious," Jacob said as he glanced up at Laura standing beside the table. "Aren't you eating?"

"Huh! I ate hours ago, while you two lingered in bed." Her eyebrows shot up, not even trying to conceal her thoughts this time, but Jacob knew she was joking.

Jacob reached out and clasped Clarissa's hand grinning at her. "I don't mind if we do," he said, amusement evident in his voice. "We are newlyweds, after all."

Laura busied herself pouring coffee for the pair.

"What shall we do today? As I mentioned earlier, a tour of the ranch would be nice, just to give you an idea of the place."

"That sounds good. What time is the driver booked to collect us?"

Jacob stared at her, his gaze piercing her very soul. Then he grinned. "Oh, I get it now. You're making a joke."

Why would her husband think she was joking? When she decided to flee her family home, she arranged a time for the driver to collect her. He arrived at the precise time she'd given him. Why would this be any different? "I, I don't understand," she said, feeling suddenly uncertain. "Are you telling me you don't have a driver?" She glanced about. Both Laura and Jacob were studying her. Until now, she hadn't detected the absence of staff other than Laura. "You don't have staff, do you?" She was feeling a little light-headed at the news.

"We have Laura, but she is more like family than staff, she's been with us so long."

She glanced across at the housekeeper. Pity was written all over her face. She probably thought Clarissa was a spoiled brat from a rich home, and she'd be right. She had not lifted a finger her entire life. She'd never even chosen her clothes for the day. Daisy, her maid had done that for her each morning after she woke her mistress from sleep.

She would open the blinds and draw a bath for Clarissa, and she would soak in it for nearly an hour before Daisy returned to help her dry off and dress. She would then brush and style Clarissa's hair.

She swallowed down the lump in her throat realizing she had left that life behind when she fled. Worse still, her marriage to Jacob had been consummated, so there was no turning back. Tears suddenly filled her eyes. Clarissa was not one to cry, but she felt overwhelmed at the situation she now found herself in.

"It's not that bad," Jacob said, his handing rubbing across her back.

This total stranger who was her husband thought he knew how she felt? "Isn't it?" Her heart pounded, her head hurt, and she turned fleeing the room. Clarissa found herself outside the front door, taking deep breaths, and trying to calm herself. What she would do now, she had no idea. But she couldn't stay here. Couldn't stay married to Jacob. Her entire world had come crashing down around her, and her life was in ruins.

"I, I don't understand any of this," Jacob told Laura. "Why is she so upset?"

Laura studied him. "Clarissa has obviously come from a highly prosperous family. What don't you understand?" She appeared annoyed at him, and Jacob wasn't sure why. It wasn't his fault his wife didn't know what she was getting herself into. Besides, it was Clarissa who was desperate to marry. He was happy to wait until the right person came along. Teddy said they suited each other. In fact, he'd insisted. Said they were the perfect couple and if he waited, she would be snapped up. He even told Jacob there were several highly unsuitable men on the sidelines wanting to marry her.

Jacob should have realized there was more to it than what Teddy had told him. The family lawyer was cunning, that was for sure. He was used to manipulating people to get the outcome he wanted. Well, he'd certainly done that this time.

"Go after her, Jacob. Don't just sit there." Laura sounded quite annoyed now, and he turned to glare at her, but paused. This wasn't Laura's fault, and it wasn't his. It certainly wasn't Clarissa's fault either. If anyone was to blame it was Teddy for not telling either of them the full story. In particular, his wife should have been given more information. After all, she was the one who was taking several steps down from her station in life.

Jacob took a restorative breath and headed to the front door. It stood open and he could see Clarissa standing outside, her back to him. She appeared stiff as a board and was undoubtedly upset. He wasn't sure what to say to her. *Too bad, we're already married,* didn't seem appropriate. Jacob shook himself. He was not a cruel person and prided himself on being caring and kind. Did his wife see him that way? He might not ever know if she chose to leave. But where would she go? That was probably the question crossing her mind. Truth be told, Jacob didn't want her to leave.

She held tightly to the wooden fence that surrounded the *Broken Arrow* mansion. At least he'd always thought of it as a mansion, even when he and his brothers were children and the whole family lived here. No doubt it was a cottage in Clarissa's eyes. He wished he knew her situation before she'd arrived. At least he might have been able to give her fair warning. This way it had been foisted on her when it was all too late.

He stood in the doorway and stared at her shaking back. Her sobs wracking the air broke his heart. "Clarissa." She turned to face him. Her eyes were red and puffy, and her expression sad. She turned away from him again. He strode the few steps to reach her and pulled his bride into his arms. At first, she tried to pull away, but he enveloped her firmly, stopping her premature escape. Finally, she leaned her head against his chest. The sobs had subsided, but tears streamed down her face. His beautiful wife was a disaster, but he felt nothing except compassion for her.

They needed to find a way to sort this mess out, unfortunately Jacob wasn't sure that was even possible.

The pair stood silently, wrapped in each other's arms for what seemed forever. Finally, Clarissa stared up at him, and tried to pull away, but Jacob wasn't ready to let her go just yet. She was still very upset. "I'm sorry," she said quietly. "That should not have happened. If Mother were here now, she would be appalled at my very public display."

Is that what she thought? That this was an appalling display? He felt sad for what she must have endured in her life. Emotions and feelings were not meant to be suppressed. His hand seemed to have a mind of its own and rubbed circles over her back. "There is nothing for you to be sorry about," he said gently. "Teddy should have explained better."

"Yes, he should have." She pursed her lips as though trying to stem her anger. "Why did he do this to me? To us?"

She settled back against his chest, and Jacob tightened his arms around her. He was happy with their union, felt a connection with Clarissa. She was the one who'd felt the brunt of Teddy's deception, and it wasn't fair. Did he do it to stop her from marrying someone highly unsuitable? Perhaps even someone cruel. He liked to think so. Teddy had always looked out for Jacob and his brothers. He'd arranged each of their marriages, and until now, had organized a perfect match.

Not that he could say Clarissa wasn't a perfect match for him. Jacob was more than happy with the wife Teddy had chosen for him. He wasn't sure Clarissa would say the same.

Chapter Four

After a hot bath, Clarissa felt far better. Jacob had been comforting and reassuring – exactly what she needed at the time. He'd tried to convince her they would work it out, and in time, she would be happy being married to him.

She wasn't sure whether he was trying to convince her, or himself.

He seemed like the perfect husband, which is what Teddy had told her. What he didn't say was that she would be taking a giant leap down from her present station in life. She would probably never forgive him for that.

Clarissa stepped out of the bath and reached for the luxurious towel Laura had placed there for her. The lavender oil added to the bubble bath had calmed her and made her feel far better than she had before. Jacob said he would be in the parlor waiting, but also told her to take her time. She couldn't wish for a better husband.

She wrapped herself in the towel and stared at her image in the mirror. The cold water Laura suggested Clarissa splash on her face had almost restored her eyes to normal. Her embarrassment at her emotional display would probably never leave her.

Just thinking about her behavior almost brought her to tears again, but Clarissa would not allow that to happen. These were kind people she found herself amongst, and she would not let them think otherwise.

"Do you need anything," Laura called through the bathroom door. "Let me know if you do."

For the first time in her life, Clarissa had privacy. Laura hadn't barged into the room without knocking, only to find her standing there stark naked. Jacob hadn't stared down at her in the tub while she bathed either. It was certainly a nice turn of events. "Thank you, I'm fine. I'm just getting dried." As she said the words, Clarissa realized this was probably the first time in her entire life she'd dried herself after a bath. It had certainly been a day of firsts for her.

~*~

"You don't do physical work? What do you do then?" She asked the question as they wandered across the field toward the barn.

Jacob had just finished explaining he had a foreman and cowpokes who worked his land. Even as a young boy he hadn't been interested in that side of his father's business, he was more about the paperwork. The accounting side of things. So much so, his now deceased father had sent him away to learn the correct way to do things. It was the best thing Father had ever done for him.

Of course, there had been a time he was expected to work the land. There was a long history of his ancestors working the land. According to the ledgers he had found in his father's study, this very land had been in the hands of Adams' men for centuries, and Jacob would ensure it would stay that way for years to come.

The entire *Broken Arrow* ranch was divided into three shares. Each brother had an equal share, but they helped each other out when needed. They all had their own workers, and their own homes. When they were given their share of the land many years ago, Noah and Seth decided they each wanted to build a home on their own property rather than stay in the main house. When their families came along, as they now had, the brothers wanted their privacy. Given he was now married, Jacob finally understood their demand for privacy.

"Not everyone is interested in physical work. Did your father do that type of work?" The words were out before he could stop them. They weren't meant in malice but said out of curiosity. Given she'd already been upset today, Jacob wished he had bitten his tongue.

She gazed up at him. "You're right, I'm sorry. I just assumed…"

"Because it's a ranch, you assumed I'd work the land, right?"

Clarissa nodded.

"I do the bookwork for all three properties. My brothers pay a small fee for me to do what they hate doing." He grinned at her trying to lift the heavy cloud that had surrounded them. He didn't want pettiness to come between them; they'd had enough of that earlier today. "And I pay my workers to do what I hate doing." He reached out and took her hand. She stared down at their now entwined hands, then glanced up at him.

Then she smiled. It lit up her incredibly beautiful face, and a shiver went down his spine. "This is the barn," he said, trying to get his mind back to where it should be. "Floyd is my foreman. He's also my cousin and oversees my property." He looked down at her shoes, then glanced at the mess on the ground. "I don't think we should go in there. Neither of us are wearing appropriate footwear."

She raised her eyebrows. "Have you ever gone in there?" she asked teasingly.

Jacob chuckled. "Well, no. I guess I haven't."

"It rather smells too," Clarissa said, screwing up her nose.

He took a deep breath to clarify what she said. Clarissa was right. "I think we should leave," he said, grinning again. He squeezed her hand, and she didn't complain.

"Hello, Boss. Missus." A cowpoke wandered out of the barn as they turned to leave. "Did you want to take a look around? I was just mucking out the stalls."

Jacob introduced his wife to the newcomer. "How are you doing, Chance? This is Clarissa, my wife."

The other man raised his eyebrows at the pair. "Congratulations," he said, his expression questioning, but not saying another word. "If you don't need me, I'll get back to it." He nodded, then strolled back into the barn.

"See that cottage in the distance," Jacob asked, pointing to his right as they walked away. "That's where Floyd, my foreman lives. The other cottages further down are the other worker's cottages. Floyd's brother Karl works here too. Each man has his own home. I respect their right to privacy," Jacob said. "Floyd and Karl are my cousins.

Chance, who you just met, lives in one of those cottages too."

"I like that each one has their own home," she said, smiling up at him. "It shows how much you care."

That small gesture set his heart to racing, and Jacob wanted to pull her close, but was sure his wife would not be pleased if he did that out here where everyone could see. He glanced around; they were totally alone. *Should he take a chance?* His heart still beating wildly, Jacob didn't give it a second thought. Instead, he pulled Clarissa close against him. "I like holding you like this," he said, glancing down at her. She didn't try to pull away, so Jacob decided she must like it too. It warmed his heart.

"We shouldn't be doing this out here," she whispered, although no one was around to hear her.

Despite her words, Clarissa leaned in close, wrapping her arms around his waist. Jacob liked being married and hoped Clarissa did too. He was certain that given time, the two might even fall in love. He glanced down at her; she seemed happy to be there with him, but only time would tell. Could the two eventually fall in love, or was that a wish that could never come true? After all, she was here under duress. Had her parents not died, and if her brothers hadn't tried to marry her off to some evil rich mogul, she would be safe at home right now.

Jacob's arms tightened around her. He felt as though he needed to hold her close in case she decided to leave. He shook off the thought. She had nowhere else to go, and no money. His mind ticked over. He needed to fix that right now. He would set up an allowance so that Clarissa never felt she had to stay, even if he did want her here. Even if she left him, the allowance would continue. Jacob did not want his wife to feel beholden to him. Not ever. He wanted her to be independent and happy, and to able to purchase whatever she wanted or needed. He would set up an allowance immediately.

Chance held the horses as Jacob helped his wife up onto the buggy. As they headed to church, he wondered about her clothes. He wasn't one to follow fashion, especially women's fashion, but felt she was quite overdressed for the service. He would ask his sisters-in-law to take Clarissa to town and help her choose more suitable clothing for her new location. The last thing he wanted was for his wife to stand out and make her feel uncomfortable.

He admitted today would be difficult for her. She would meet his brothers and their wives for the first time. He hadn't told any of them he'd married by proxy as he'd wanted to surprise them. Halliwell didn't have a large population, but when everyone got together, as they did on Sundays, it could be quite overwhelming to a newcomer.

Glancing across as he flicked the reins, Jacob noticed her fiddling with her bonnet. He guessed Clarissa would be nervous, but this confirmed it. Coming from her background, he was almost certain she would be admonished for adjusting her bonnet in public. For Jacob it was not a problem, but he understood the guilt she would be feeling. "You look perfect. Your bonnet is perfect too." He smiled at her, hoping to make his wife feel more at ease. She glanced about as though she was seeing the area for the first time. He realized she was likely to upset on her way here to take much notice of the surrounding area when she arrived.

"That's Seth's place," he said pointing. "And that's Noah's place over there. You'll get to meet them this morning." He watched as she placed her hands daintily on her lap, but her fidgeting fingers gave her away. "Don't be nervous. No one will bite you."

Instead of grinning as he'd expected, she bit her bottom lip. "You do attend church, don't you?" He had to wonder if he was taking her to a place she dreaded.

"Of course," she said quickly. "I'm…anxious about meeting your family. Why didn't you tell them you'd married?"

"I wanted to surprise them."

"You will certainly do that," she said softly. "I'd annoyed if you were my brother." When he glanced at her again, all color had drained from her face. *Was she missing her family? Even after they'd tried to force her into a marriage she didn't want?*

He reached over and covered her hand. "Are you all right? You've gone quite pale."

She lifted her chin in defiance and turned to face him. "I'm fine. I, I, I miss my mother." Her voice broke and she turned away from him, then brushed at her cheek. Jacob squeezed her hand. "I'm sorry," he said gently. He slowed the buggy almost to a walking pace, then pulled to the side of the road. "Do you want to go back home? I don't mind, I promise." Jacob felt like a heel. It had been little more than a week since she'd lost both parents. Soon after, she'd had to marry by proxy or be forced to marry someone she despised. Life had not been kind to his wife lately.

Jacob scurried across the seat and put an arm around her. Clarissa stiffened her back and turned away from him. A hand came up and wiped at her cheek again. She was crying but didn't want him to see. That was sad. He wondered what her life had been like growing up. Had her childhood been happy, or had Clarissa been forced into acting like a machine rather than a child? It hurt his heart to even think about it.

"Everything all right, Boss?" Jacob turned to see Floyd, his foreman astride his horse. He had pulled alongside the buggy.

"We're fine. I'm not sure if we'll make it. Clarissa is feeling a little…unwell." When he glanced at her, his wife had pursed her lips. She obviously wasn't happy at his declaration.

"I am perfectly all right," she said, her words stiff. "We'll be along shortly." She lifted her chin again, and Jacob was beginning to see a whole different side to her. It was all he could do not to grin.

He glanced at Floyd and lifted his eyebrows. "Apparently we'll be along shortly."

His foreman grinned and went on his way again. This being married was tricky stuff. Jacob might have to get some pointers from his brothers. After they calmed down from being kept in the dark, that was.

The service was about to start when they arrived, and they slid into the back row. With both his brothers having young families, they were close to the back as well. That way they could slip out quietly, should the need arise. Everyone stood as the first hymn began. Jacob put an arm around Clarissa and felt her entire body shaking. He tightened his grip around her. Should they leave, or would it be better to let her calm down? After all, the Lord's house was the best place he could think of for a person to take their worries. She turned to face him, and their eyes met. It was plain to see she was troubled. Jacob hoped she would feel comfortable talking to him about her concerns. Or perhaps she might feel better with Preacher Joe? Either way, his wish was for his wife to feel more relaxed in her surroundings.

Everyone sat and Jacob clasped his father's bible. It was well worn, and in truth, he probably should replace it. But it was the last emotional connection he had to his father, and he didn't want to let it go.

"Today's reading is from Jeremiah 29:11," Preacher Joe said, and Jacob quickly opened his bible and followed along with the words before him. *"'For I know the plans I have for you,'"* Preacher Joe began.

Jacob's heart rate quickened as the words continued. It was as though the Lord was speaking directly to him. He immediately knew Clarissa had been chosen for him, and Jacob for her. Was he meant to save her from the fate her brothers had planned without her permission? He was beginning to believe that was the case.

His faith had always been strong, but today, the reading felt as though it was meant for him, and perhaps even for his wife. A shiver went down his spine.

"Let us pray," Preacher Joe said, then everyone kneeled and began to recite the Lord's Prayer. By the time they'd finished, Jacob felt completely overwhelmed. Something had changed. Shifted. His heart felt far more full than it had been before they arrived. He suddenly had a purpose, a reason for living. And that purpose was Clarissa. As her husband, it was up to him to support her through her grief and help her become a firm part of his life. His family's life.

He wouldn't force her to stay, but with God's help, he would endeavor to show her she was a valued and vital member of his family and was loved.

Chapter Five

Clarissa's heart thudded as she was introduced to Jacob's family after church. Their shock showed on their faces, but they seemed to accept her. The warmth they'd already shown her was more than her own siblings had afforded her for most of their lives, and already Clarissa felt welcomed.

Just like that she had an entirely new family, and was suddenly an aunt to three youngsters – Eugene who was barely walking, five-year-old Mabel, and baby Marcus. Jacob stood by her side the entire time, which she appreciated. The one thing Clarissa didn't do well was mingle with strangers. They might now be her family, but in essence, Jacob's brothers and sisters-in-law were still outsiders to her. Hopefully that would change soon. She'd only been on the ranch a short time, and already she felt isolated. Knowing there were two other women in the same situation helped somewhat, and Clarissa hoped she would get to know them better over time.

"Clarissa needs a whole new wardrobe," Jacob suddenly blurted out, and she glared at him. Abigail and Mary, her sisters-in-law glanced at the gown she was wearing. They nodded in agreement.

"I can spare time tomorrow," Abigail said, then turned to Mary, her expression questioning.

Mary grinned. "I can make time tomorrow. It will be so much fun." The two women glanced at each other, then at Clarissa. "We could pick you up at…"

"Ten," Abigail finished, then rubbed her hands together as much as she could with a baby in her arms. "Laura might be kind enough to babysit for a few hours?"

Jacob grinned. "I'm sure she will relish the opportunity. We know how much she loves children. Besides I can help out if necessary."

The two women glanced at each other conspiratorially; it seemed they didn't believe he was up to the task. If she was honest, neither did Clarissa. Although to give him credit, she'd never seen him with children before today.

"That's settled then," Abigail suddenly said. "We'll pick you up at ten. We'll make a day of it and have lunch in Halliwell. Assuming our husbands have no objection." She stared at each man one by one, daring them to challenge her. Not one did. It took all Clarissa's effort not to grin. It seemed Abigail was a woman after her own heart, and she knew they were going to become great friends.

"She needs a complete wardrobe," Jacob suddenly announced. "And boots. Nothing Clarissa has brought with her is suitable for the ranch."

Her heart thudded, but she knew he was right. She glanced down at her feet; the boots she wore were more suitable for dancing than traipsing around on a grassy paddock. Her gown was fit for the most exclusive ball rather than attending church or even pottering around the house, but it was all she had. Each and every item in her wardrobe was unsuitable, and had she known, she would have left them all behind instead of giving the stagecoach driver the burden of their weight.

On second thought, she wouldn't give her brother the satisfaction. He would have either handed them off to his egocentric wife, who would have flinched at the thought of second-hand anything or donated them to the poor. That would have been like winning the lottery to some unfortunate soul, and it made her wish she had left everything behind after all.

Abigail suddenly hooked her arm through Clarissa's and the three women headed to the front of the church hall, on a mission for refreshments. The children were safely with their fathers. Jacob had a lovely family, a close-knit family, and she relished it. Perhaps one day she and Jacob might have a child of their own.

But she was getting ahead of herself. First, she had to decide whether or not she would stay. The way she felt right now, the possibility was low, but she had the distinct feeling her sisters-in-law might convince her to stay – not by their words, but by their actions.

The three women chatted all the way into Halliwell, exchanging stories of how they became proxy brides. Clarissa had thought she was desperate, but now realized her situation was far from dire compared to these two ladies who were now her family. She felt ashamed of herself for the way she'd behaved when she discovered there were no servants in the house.

Her father had told her repeatedly she was a spoiled brat, but Clarissa was certain he was wrong. He'd now been proven right, but it didn't make her feel any better. She could easily blame her parents, for they were the ones who brought her up that way, but she knew the onus was really on her. She had relished having servants run after her, she'd adored the attention from the young gentlemen who rallied around her, even if she didn't want to marry, and she loved getting expensive gifts from her parents. But most of all, she adored the fact her father was the richest man in Helena, even if she didn't have direct access to that money.

Her brother had stopped her allowance the moment he found out she'd married by proxy, but truth be told, what she received each month was probably more money than Mary and Abigail had seen in their entire lives. Clarissa felt the self-loathing set in. She had squandered most of that money when she could have donated it to the church to help those in desperate circumstances.

The thought made her pause. Jacob told her he was setting up an allowance for her, but now she wasn't so sure she wanted it. His generosity was more than she deserved, but she understood his thinking, and appreciated it. She listened carefully as he explained that even if she left him, the allowance would continue. The memory of that moment returned now. Understanding she would never want for anything, despite no longer being married to him, should that happen, was reassuring.

Jacob was a kind and generous man, and she owed it to him to at least give their marriage a chance and not rush into anything. After all, they'd only been together for a number of days, and that wasn't nearly long enough to know if it would work.

"We've arrived." Mary's voice brought her out of her dark thoughts, and Clarissa glanced up. In large gold letters *Daphne's Designs* was written across the large window.

Abigail and Mary piled out of the buggy, so Clarissa followed suit. She took a deep restorative breath. The last time she went clothing shopping was with her mother, but that time it was for custom clothing that cost an outrageous amount of money. Enough to feed all the needy in Halliwell, she guessed. Guilt overtook her. "I, I don't think I can do this," she said, her heart pounding. "It will cost far too much."

Her sisters-in-law stared at her. "Well, you can't go around wearing gowns meant for highfalutin balls," Abigail told her in no uncertain terms. "Daphne will outfit you for far less than the cost of that one gown, I guarantee it."

Was that right? She had no reason to mistrust Abigail, so surely she told the truth. "If you're certain."

"We are," the two women told her at the same time.

"Don't worry," Mary said gently. "We went through the same feelings of guilt you are experiencing."

"We have done what you're doing now. Let us help you through it."

Clarissa nodded warily. The difference was she had come from a far different background from the women who stood before her now. She was only now coming to realize what a privileged existence she'd had, and how much money had been wasted on her. Sure, Jacob could afford to outfit her in new, more suitable clothes, but she didn't want to spend his money, especially when she may not stay married to him.

The thought brought her emotions to the core, and she swallowed. A shudder ran down her spine at the mere thought of what might happen to her should she decide to leave.

As though she could read her mind, Abigail grabbed her by the hand and pulled Clarissa inside. She glanced about at the seemingly endless racks of clothing scattered around the walls and in the middle of the store. There were curtains at the back of the room, presumably for customers to try on the clothing. It was rather dark, with the only light coming from the large window at the front.

"This is Clarissa, Jacob's new wife," she told the salesclerk. "She needs a whole new wardrobe of clothes."

The other woman reached out her hand. "Nice to meet you, Clarissa. I'm Daphne." Her hand was soft and warm, and Clarissa felt immediately welcomed to this quaint little store. It was a genuine welcome too, unlike what she'd experienced in Helena, where all the storekeeper was interested in was her father's money.

"I'm pleased to meet you too, Daphne," she said quietly, not feeling very confident about this entire expedition. "Apparently I need new clothes." She glanced down at the gown she was wearing, which Clarissa had to admit was far from suitable for a little country town.

Daphne pulled out her tape measure and jotted down some measurements, then glanced about the store. Her eyes suddenly opened in excitement. "I had a new shipment a few days ago, and I have just the right gowns for you." She scurried across to a rack on the opposite side of the room.

Mary and Abigail giggled, then pulled her toward the rack Daphne had stopped at. "Oh, they're beautiful," Mary exclaimed. "You must try them on." She pulled out one of the gowns, but Clarissa screwed up her face is dismay. The quality of these gowns was not what she was used to wearing. *But wasn't that exactly why she was here?*

Daphne glanced at her but continued pulling several gowns off the rack despite her display. "These will look perfect on you, Clarissa. Come with me and we'll check them for size."

She stood where she was, but Mary and Abigail gently pushed her forward. "This is so much fun,"

Abigail said, and Clarissa realized she would spoil their entire day if she didn't comply. She had always been a loner, and rarely spent time with others, except for her father's servants. Daisy was the exception, as she hovered around Clarissa almost the entire day, ensuring her mistress was happy and well looked after. The young woman was close to Clarissa's age, and she was the nearest to a friend Clarissa had. It made her wonder what happened to Daisy now that Clarissa was gone.

Daphne carefully helped her out of her gown, hanging it carefully, then assisted as she tried on one of the gowns she had chosen for her new customer. "Just as I suspected," she said. "The color suits you perfectly." She turned Clarissa to face the full-length mirror. "What do you think?"

She stared at her image in disbelief. The pale blue of the gown did suit her, far better than the gawdy gold gown she had been wearing. The rounded neck with white lace sat gently above the feminine styled bodice that tapered at the waist, then gathered in and fell beautifully to the ground. The sleeves had matching white lace and were ruffled to match.

She drew in a breath, and Daphne stared at her in the mirror. "You don't like it?" Disappointment clouded her features.

"Totally the opposite," Clarissa told her. "I love it, and the color is perfect."

A grin broke out on the storekeeper's face, and she breathed a sigh of relief. "Thank goodness. For a moment there I thought you hated it." She reached for another gown. "The size is perfect too." Daphne threw the curtain back to allow Mary and Abigail check it out.

After some ooohs and aaahs, they insisted on her taking that gown. Not that Clarissa needed much cajoling. After that she tried several other gowns, each one perfect. Daphne helped her choose two pair of boots, and a few accessories she was likely to need. All in all, they spent nearly two hours at *Daphne's Designs*, but the time seemed to pass in a whirl. She hadn't had so much fun in a very long time.

She chose to wear the pale blue gown, the first one she'd tried on, for the remainder of the day. They would now go to lunch, and Daphne promised to have everything boxed up ready to take home when they returned. Her purchases were all added to Jacob's account.

As the three women strolled arm in arm toward the *Halliwell Diner*, Clarissa suddenly felt as though she now had the sisters she'd never had. Oh, she had three blood sisters, but they'd never done much together. Her sisters had always treated her with contempt, likely because she was the eldest sister and was treated differently than the younger girls.

They were also forced into marriage, where she'd defied her parents and refused.

It wasn't her fault she stood her ground where they wilted like fading flowers. *Was it?* Of course it wasn't, and she had no need to feel the slightest bit guilty over the decisions they'd made.

As they were seated, she was certain her relationship with Mary and Abigail would be much different to that with her sisters. They were open and friendly, and despite having met her only yesterday, Clarissa felt as though they cared about her. She had never got that feeling from her blood sisters.

As she was handed a menu, Clarissa knew if she only gave her marriage a chance, she could have a good life with these wonderful ladies. The placed their orders, then the conversation turned to their husbands and children.

Clarissa had the feeling she had finally come home.

Chapter Six

It had been a wonderful day, and Clarissa didn't want it to end. But finish it must, because Laura and Jacob were caring for the three children. She was certain Laura would cope, but Jacob was a whole different kettle of fish. He might be the children's uncle, but that didn't mean he had an inkling of how to care for them.

She threw back the front door, her arms full of packages, and headed toward the bedroom. She heard giggling coming from the parlor. As the three women approached the parlor, she heard Mabel call out. "Aunty! I missed you!" The five year old slammed into Abigail who had a broad smile on her face.

What she would give to have someone greet her so passionately. She tucked her head around the door, and noticed Jacob sat holding baby Marcus. He stared down into the baby's face longingly, and Clarissa wondered if he yearned for his own child. It wasn't something she'd given a lot of thought, but being a married woman now, and sharing a bed with her husband meant the possibility was certainly there.

Jacob glanced up and saw her studying him. A wide smile broke onto his face, and warmth flooded her. Had he missed her? She'd had so much fun today she hadn't given him much of a thought, which was a horrid way to think, but it was the truth. Mary and Abigail had been so welcoming, and so supportive, and she had blocked out all other thoughts as much as she could.

"Did you have a good day?" Jacob stood with the baby still in his arms, and he looked like he'd been doing it forever. He seemed so comfortable and looked very nurturing, and it warmed her heart. Abigail glanced from one to the other of them, then relieved Jacob of her son.

"I did. It was thoroughly enjoyable." He stepped toward her and put an arm around her shoulder. A shudder went through her. *Why did she react so much to his touch?* They were virtual strangers and yet his touch affected her beyond comprehension. He glanced down into her face, and for a brief moment she was certain he was going to kiss her. Right here in the middle of the parlor with everyone watching!

At the last moment he glanced about as if finally remembering they had an audience. Not that Clarissa thought it would bother Abigail or Mary, and when she looked, they were both grinning. Even Mabel thought it funny. The child was giggling and had her hands to her mouth. Clarissa felt the heat rising up in her face, and pulled out of his grip, turning away from everyone in the room, lest they notice.

As if just noticing she wore one of her purchases, Jacob remarked on its beauty. "You look lovely," he said. "The color suits you."

"It really does," Abigail said, noticing Clarissa's discomfit. "We both told her that. Daphne found some beautiful gowns that suit her perfectly." She grabbed Mabel by the hand. "We'd best get moving," she said, heading for the front door. "Thank you for looking after the children today, Laura. You too, Jacob." Truth be known, Jacob was of little help, if any.

"It is always a pleasant day when children are involved," Laura replied. "I miss rearing little ones." She glanced across first at Jacob and then Clarissa. *Was she sending a not so subtle message to them both?* It was in the hands of the Lord, and neither one of them had a say in it. As if reading her mind, Jacob pulled Clarissa to him and grinned. She wanted to vanish into the floor.

A grin on her face, Abigail pushed past them toward the front door. Mary collected Eugene and followed suit. Laura pushed past them too. Before long, the newlyweds were alone. This time when Jacob leaned into her, he kissed her tenderly on the lips. A shudder went through her even at such a gentle touch. "I missed you today," he said quietly.

If she hadn't been so surprised by his kiss, she might have been more shocked by his words. Did Jacob really mean what he said, or was he doing all he could to try and entice her to stay? She would probably never know, but she had to admit it felt nice being held in his arms.

"Thank you." She said the words quietly, not knowing what else to say.

He stared down at her. "For what? I've haven't done anything."

She glanced down at her new gown. "For the new clothes," she said flicking her gown briefly. "And the boots, and well…making me feel wanted."

He stared into her eyes, and she couldn't pull her gaze from his. Teddy was right – Jacob was a kind and genuine person. He didn't deserve someone like herself who was so ungrateful of his generosity. She needed to make a decision to stay or leave.

Jacob tried to concentrate on the paperwork in front of him, but thoughts of Clarissa went through his mind. It had been a little over a week since she'd arrived unannounced, but already he had feelings for her. His gut told him those feelings weren't reciprocated, and it broke his heart.

It was clear she had never had a real connection with her family but seeing her interactions with Abigail and Mary gave him hope. They had both visited with the children twice more since their visit to town, which was unheard of. In the past, it was rare for them to visit his home, but now they had reason to come around. Warmth spread through him at the thought.

It had been several days since she'd mentioned leaving, but the possibility sat at the back of his mind, eating away at him. Jacob didn't want her to leave. Besides, where would she go? At least here on the *Broken Arrow Ranch* she was wanted and loved.

That thought made him pause. *Was he in love with Clarissa?* Surely after such a short time it was impossible, but it truly was how he felt. He could hear her pottering about with Laura in the kitchen. His wife had become bored rather quickly on the days they didn't have visitors, so the housekeeper had taken Clarissa under her wing. She was teaching Clarissa the basics of cooking, but Jacob did not have high expectations. Not yet anyway. When you'd had servants your entire life, there was no incentive to learn.

He tried to shake his unwanted thoughts away, and went back to the paperwork in front of him. There were accounts to settle and figures to be clarified. Normally he relished working with numbers, but today they danced in front of his eyes and Jacob couldn't concentrate. He shut the ledgers and decided to call it day. Closing the study door, he was about to head to the kitchen for coffee when the sound of something smashing caught his attention. He hurried toward the noise when he heard a scream. His wife was injured, he was convinced of it. His heart fluttered and he began to run.

Jacob came to a sudden halt in the doorway to the large kitchen. A shattered glass dish lay spread across the floor. The two women were crouched on the floor, their backs to him. He cautiously came around to check what was happening. His heart pounded at the scene before him.

Laura held a kitchen towel to his wife's hand. Was she badly injured? As blood seeped through the towel, he had his answer. Jacob crouched down to their level to check for himself. "How bad is it?" he asked, his voice breaking. He'd always been good in a crisis, so this was new to him. He lifted the kitchen towel and gasped. The cut was deep, and he was certain it would need stitches. He had to keep his panic in check – the last thing he wanted to do was upset Clarissa. "I'll send one of the men for the doc."

Laura stared at him. "That would waste too much time. This needs stitches now. Floyd can do it. He stitches the animals when it's needed."

Jacob mentally slapped himself. *Why didn't he think of that?* He glanced up at Clarissa. Her eyes were shimmering with tears. *Was she in pain?* Stupid question, of course she was. A cut that deep had to hurt. Without saying a word, he helped her to her feet and led her to the parlor, where he sat her down.

"I'm sorry," she said quietly.

He gazed into her face that was etched with worry. "For what?"

She pulled her gaze away from him and stared down into her lap. "For breaking the dish."

She was apologizing for breaking a dish? He was worried about her, not some blasted dish that was easily replaced. "It's nothing. I'll fetch Floyd. Will you be all right here?"

Clarissa nodded and he left her with Laura, so he knew she was in safe hands.

Floyd rushed into the room, a first aid kit in his hands. He looked flustered, which worried Clarissa. *Had he stitched people before, or only horses and cows?* The thought terrified her.

"It looks bad, Jacob," Floyd said, as he checked the wound. "Are you sure you want me to do this? The doc might be better." Nonetheless he opened up the first aid kit and pulled out some bandages along with needle and thread.

Jacob stood next to her and nodded. Floyd prepared for the minor surgery.

The laudanum Laura had given her had relieved some of the pain, but Clarissa was more concerned about the amount of blood she had lost. The kitchen towel was soaked with blood, and she was now onto the second one.

"This might hurt a bit, despite the laudanum," Floyd said, glancing at the bottle sitting on the side table. She stiffened but didn't say a word. Jacob sat on the arm of the chair and put an arm around her. She felt very comforted despite her dire situation. Clarissa leaned into him and closed her eyes. When she opened them again, she was lying in bed with Jacob sitting on the bed next to her, concern written all over his face.

She lifted her injured hand – it was bandaged, and despite the severity, there was little pain. "Floyd did a great job stitching your hand," Jacob told her. He reached across and held her other hand and she felt strangely comforted. It was then she realized Jacob was always there when she needed him. He was her protector, but more than that, he cared for her, which was more than she'd felt from her own family since her parents had died.

She had been an annoyance who was in the way of her brothers earning money from the house sale. They couldn't wait to be rid of her, and clearly didn't care what happened to her. Marrying her off to someone rich, albeit repulsive, meant she was off their hands, and no longer their worry.

Jacob was different. He genuinely cared about her, even if it was only because she lived here as his wife. She doubted there would ever be love between them, especially since theirs was an arranged marriage. Her parents had an arranged marriage, and despite producing nine children, she had never seen anything that amounted to love between the two. Her mother had married into money by arrangement, and that was the end of the story. Rich married rich, and that was how it had always been.

Mother had told her in no uncertain terms that when she eventually married, and Mother knew she would, she would live a good life with someone of the same social standing. It seemed to be the only thing her parents cared about – that their son-in-law was on equal grounding as the filthy rich Reyes of Helena.

She closed her eyes at the thought, but the vision did not leave her. In fact, it was worse. When she finally opened them again, Jacob was gone, no doubt thinking she was asleep. The realization that she wanted him here next to her was inconceivable. All this time she had thought she didn't want to be married to Jacob, and now she was doubting herself. Or was it the laudanum doing her thinking?

Clarissa closed her eyes again, and this time she let herself sink into a deep sleep, leaving all her troubles behind her.

Chapter Seven

"Open your hand again." Doc Petersen studied Floyd's handiwork. She flinched when he touched her skin. "Floyd did a magnificent job," he said to anyone who would listen.

"He's had plenty of practice," Jacob said. "Although Clarissa was his first human patient." He chuckled, but she didn't find it at all funny but was glad she wasn't aware at the time Floyd was stitching her hand.

After he'd cleaned and bandaged her hand once more, the doc turned to her husband. "Bring your wife back in a week or so, and those stitches should be ready to come out." He smiled at Clarissa. "You should be able to use your hand normally after that. If ever I need stitches, remind me to get Floyd to do them for me." He chuckled at his own joke, but Clarissa didn't find it funny. Neither did his nurse who was busy tidying up after the doctor.

Jacob led her out the door and toward the *Halliwell Mercantile*. "We might as well make the most of our time here. After we've ordered our supplies, we can have lunch at the diner."

The moment they stepped into the mercantile they were greeted. "I heard about your accident," Elizabeth Dalton said sympathetically. "Did you get Doc Petersen to check it out?"

Clarissa understood news traveled fast in a small town, but this was the first time they'd been in Halliwell since her accident almost a week ago. It had been healing nicely, and despite his protests, she convinced Jacob to wait a little longer before she needed to see the doc. "We've just left there," she told the other woman, appreciative of her concern. They'd never met before, yet this stranger worried for her.

"Good to hear. I'm Elizabeth, by the way. Albert, my husband, is out back in the storeroom. Now what can I do for you both today?"

Elizabeth held her hand out in anticipation, and Jacob handed over the list Laura had given him. "We're going to the diner for lunch, and will collect it after that, if that's enough time."

The storekeeper scanned the list, then glanced up at Jacob. "I do believe we have most of these items, if not all. That shouldn't be a problem." She smiled then reached for a box. "Enjoy your meal."

Jacob guided her out the door and down the street. "Halliwell isn't huge, but it has everything we need."

She glanced at him. "Did you forget I've been to Halliwell before?"

At first, he looked puzzled, then his expression changed. "Of course. You came with Mary and Abigail to get a new wardrobe."

"I had a wonderful time. They are delightful women – very supportive and caring. We all get on well." Clarissa only hoped her heart would not be broken. She couldn't bear if the three of them became close, only to have her leave. It was the last thing she wanted, but she couldn't stand to think about living the rest of her life in a loveless marriage. Abigail and Mary seemed very happy with their husbands, so perhaps there was hope for her and Jacob yet. Should she dare to hope for such an outcome?

Her heart fluttered as Jacob reached for her good hand, then squeezed it gently. "I'm so happy Teddy put us together," he said quietly, and her heart soared. *Did he really mean what he said?* "I was only existing before; you have given my life meaning."

She glanced up at him, still unsure if he meant what he said. "I'm glad I came here. It's not Helena, but it's nice."

His face fell, and Clarissa immediately knew she'd offended her husband. Her words made it sound as though it was more about the town, and not about Jacob at all. "I'm sorry, I didn't mean..." But it was too late – his feelings had been hurt, and she wasn't sure she could ever fix the pain she'd caused. He helped her from the road up onto the boardwalk, and Clarissa turned to him. "I do like it here, and not just because of the town. You are a kind man, Jacob," she said, reaching out to push a stray curl from his face. "I honestly don't know where I would be today without you."

He nodded but didn't seem convinced. Clarissa glanced about and saw there were people heading toward the diner. "We can't talk now. Perhaps later, when we are alone?" More than anything she craved love. It had been sadly lacking in her life and was the one thing Clarissa had yearned for as long as she could remember.

He studied her for long moments, as though he wasn't sure what to make of her words. Then a slow smile crossed his lips, and he reached out and pulled her closer. "Of course. There's plenty of time."

Before long they were sitting in the diner, a menu in their hands, and surrounded by several other diners. It was definitely not a place for privacy.

The trip home was mostly in silence, despite them agreeing to talk later. Jacob had his mind and eyes on the road; there were far more bends and crevices along this road than he would have liked. Many a traveler had ended up down a ditch, even in the daylight.

He glanced across to see Clarissa nodding off and knew they wouldn't have their talk today. Not on their way home, anyway. Finally, she rested her head against his shoulder, and he reveled in her nearness. What he'd told her today was true. Before she arrived, he only existed. He got up in the morning, went about his work, had supper, and went to bed soon after. That pattern was continued day after day; the monotony was depressing. He'd had nothing but his work to look forward to. Of course, he had Laura to talk to, but it wasn't the same as having a wife, a companion to share your life with. Someone to share your dreams, your fears, and your nights.

Since Clarissa had arrived, he had a spring in his step. He enjoyed their short walks each day and had a new purpose in his life. His only wish was that Clarissa felt the same way, but Jacob feared she was not as committed to him as he was to her. Despite her station in life, it was clear she had never been truly loved. Not the way a child should be loved by a parent. She hadn't enjoyed the devotion one's parents should lavish on their children. Instead, she'd been lavished with worldly goods. A lot of good that had done her.

Bitterness rose up his chest and threatened to overtake him. Clarissa hadn't deserved to be treated in such a way, especially by her brothers who demanded she marry, and then banished her from her home upon discovering she had secretly married Jacob. It was appalling behavior, and her family should feel ashamed. Regrettably, he was certain they would be carefree and more concerned about the funds they would receive from the sale of her parent's home. Money begets money, as they say, and sometimes that overrides all else.

A shudder ran through him at the thought. Clarissa reached out and took his hand. "Are we home yet?"

He glanced down at her, annoyed with himself for having awoken his wife. "Not yet, but we will be soon," he said quietly. "Go back to sleep." She glanced up at him and smiled briefly, then closed her eyes again.

It had been a long day, with their trip into town taking nearly an hour each way. At least they'd had a productive day, and he'd enjoyed every moment he got to spend with his wife. He only hoped she felt the same way.

Jacob stood in the doorway to the main bedroom and watched as Clarissa brushed her hair. It was soothing observing her, just as he found her presence calming. He had come to care for his wife far more than he ever thought possible. "You look beautiful," he said quietly, and she lifted her head. A small smile crossed her features and she glanced at him through the mirror.

"You don't look so bad yourself." *Was she flirting with him?* If she was, it would have to be a first. Perhaps having the house to themselves had made her a little more game. With Laura at her knitting circle, they were totally alone for the first time since Clarissa had arrived. They had both carefully avoided the talk they'd promised each other during their visit to Halliwell. Jacob didn't want to spoil their comfortable companionship by insisting on discussing something they both found difficult.

He strolled over to where she sat at the dresser and placed his hands lightly on her shoulders. She turned her head over her shoulder toward him. Jacob leaned in and kissed her cheek. He would have been happier kissing her luscious lips but didn't want to distract her from the task at hand. Every night she sat there brushing her hair. It was a ritual that seemed to make her happy, and if Clarissa was happy, then Jacob was overjoyed. It seemed she'd endured a life with little love or caring, and it was past time she had both.

He glanced at her image in the mirror and noticed little puffs of pink coloring her cheeks. He wasn't sure if she was embarrassed by his kiss, or it was something else entirely. "Time for bed, I think," she said as she stretched her arms and yawned, but the glint in her eye told Jacob it was not sleep she yearned, but something entirely different.

She stood and he studied the embroidered linen nightgown she wore. Like everything else she'd brought with her, Clarissa's nightwear was of the highest quality, and would have cost more than a week's wages for one of his workers. It's a pity her family hadn't been so free and easy with their affection as they were with their money.

Jacob pulled her into his arms and reveled in her nearness. Why he ever thought having her here, marrying her, would be an inconvenience, he had no idea now. It was clear they were meant for each other, and he couldn't bear the thought of ever losing her.

He glanced down as she rested her head against his chest and lifted a hand to caress her back. His heart rate quickened, and warmth flooded him. She glanced up, her lips curled into a quaint little grin, and he wondered if she felt the same way.

No words passed between them, but he knew what he wanted. Jacob yearned to hold her for all eternity and never let go.

Chapter Eight

"This is so exciting!" Clarissa sat on the picnic blanket Jacob had spread out across the grass. It had been years since she'd been on a picnic. Well, one that didn't require her to keep up appearances, anyway. Most of the picnics she'd attended were for Father's benefit; something connected to the family business. The most recent one she recalled was a picnic put on for his workers. It ran an entire day so everyone could attend, even if only for a few hours.

She'd been commanded to wear one of her favorite gowns, and to look the part of heiress. A photographer came from the local newspaper and took her photograph with her father. It was all a pretense, and she'd hated every moment of it.

Clarissa still didn't see the point – everyone in Helena and beyond knew Oliver Reyes was rich beyond belief. But still he had to flaunt his riches, and more importantly, his unmarried daughter. If only he could see her now, Clarissa was certain he would be rolling over in his grave. Not only had she married below her station, but she was falling in love with the man who had saved her from a lifetime of misery.

She stared out across the vicinity of where they sat. The grass was greener than she'd noticed previously, but today she was sitting, not walking. In the distance stood a small herd of horses grazing on the luscious grass. It was so peaceful here – serene and beautiful. Clarissa almost felt as though she was living in a dream world. Jacob squeezed her hand, and she forced her thoughts back to the present. "The others should be here shortly. The children adore picnics, especially young Mabel."

"She really is a sweetheart and has had such a difficult life."

Jacob glanced her way and frowned. *Did he think she'd had a difficult life?* In many ways she had, but not like Mabel who had lost both parents in such a short period of time. The poor child had been forced to leave the only home she knew soon after her mother and new baby had died, dragged to a new town with her aunt, to live with an uncle she'd never met before. Clarissa couldn't even begin to imagine how that felt. Especially at the tender age of four. Still, she was settled now and seemed to be very happy in her new home with Abigail and Seth, and now, also baby Marcus.

Laughter made her turn her head, and Mabel came running toward them both. She wrapped her arms around Clarissa, and warmth flooded her. Mabel planted a sloppy kiss on her cheek, then she moved to Jacob and repeated the process. None of the nieces and nephews she'd left back home had ever been this affectionate. They'd been brought up to be mindful of their behavior at every turn, just as she had. The thought made Clarissa sorrowful. Of course, none of them knew any different – that was the life of the rich.

"Is Eugene coming?" The five year old glanced about looking for her young cousin, but Noah and Mary hadn't arrived yet.

"He is," Jacob answered. "They should be here soon."

Her smile lit up her little face. Mabel pushed herself between Clarissa and Jacob, content to sit and wait until her young cousin arrived. When she noticed their clasped hands, she pushed her tiny hand inside theirs too. The love this family displayed was more than anything Clarissa had ever experienced in her entire life. In the few months she'd been at *Broken Arrow*, she'd felt more wanted and cared about than she'd ever felt back in Helena. It broke her heart but warmed it at the same time.

Suddenly Mabel jumped up, almost trampling Jacob. "They're here!" Jacob grabbed her around the waist as she tried to run toward the buggy. At five, she still didn't have the capacity to understand the danger.

"What did I tell you, Mabel?" Abigail's voice was stern as she approached the picnickers. Mabel was so quick, it was hard to keep up, especially carrying a small baby.

Mabel pouted. "Sorry, Aunty." She sat back down next to Jacob, and snuggled in, duly admonished.

Abigail leaned down to Clarissa, passing her small baby over. "Would you mind? I need to get the food sorted."

"Of course not." She relished the chance to hold the tiny bundle and stared down into his face. As if he knew his mother was no longer holding him, baby Marcus suddenly opened his eyes and stared up into her face. Clarissa felt herself melt. "He's beautiful," she told Abigail. "So precious." She suddenly felt emotional but had no idea why.

Jacob glanced across at her and grinned. "You look very comfortable with a baby in your arms."

Her eyes opened in surprise. *Did he mean what she thought her husband meant?* They'd never discussed the possibility of children, though of course she knew it could happen. That decision was totally in God's hands and wasn't a choice for anyone else. Jacob continued to grin, and Clarissa pulled the baby closer to herself. She could do this, she was certain she could.

"Thanks." She glanced up to see Abigail standing there, her arms outstretched to take back her baby.

For a moment Clarissa felt protective of Marcus, as though he was *her* child and not Abigail's. She didn't know what had come over her. She'd never felt this way before and had never even contemplated the prospect of having a child of her own. But now? Her heart was unexpectedly aching. It was as though holding her nephew had opened a door to the possibility. She wondered what Jacob though of the idea.

As his mother took the baby in her arms, Jacob leaned into her and spoke quietly. "It looks good on you." Their eyes met, and his message seemed perfectly clear.

Clarissa's hands went to her stomach, and her heart pounded. *Could she be a mother?* She had no idea what that entailed since her own mother was never the mothering type. Besides, she had servants for that. She did however have Mary and Abigail, and was certain they would teach her everything she needed to know. Laura was certain to help as well. She was after all, governess to the three boys when they were young.

Jacob reached out and covered her hand which still sat on her stomach. He brought it to his lips and kissed it. "All in good time," he said softly, then leaned in and kissed her briefly on the lips.

"Eeewwww!" Mabel's sweet voice carried across to everyone there, resulting in a lot of laughter. With her days now filled with love and laughter, Clarissa had no idea why she had even contemplated leaving *Broken Arrow*. This is where she belonged, and this is where she would stay.

If Jacob would let her.

The afternoon went quickly by. Floyd joined them, along with his brother Karl who also worked on the property. Despite her protests to the contrary, Laura joined them as well, bringing a large basket of blueberry muffins with her. Clarissa glanced about. Her heart was filled with joy. So many people, and not one of them forced to be there.

She was introduced to Chance for the first time. He originally worked for Jacob's father, Barnabas, and had been there for many years now. He glanced about and settled himself next to Laura on the picnic blanket. The two seemed rather cozy, and it got Clarissa to thinking. They were around the same age and had both lived on the property for many years. *Could there be more to it?* She shook herself mentally at the inappropriate thoughts she was having.

Jacob had previously told her they were like one big happy family, and she now saw the proof for herself. Noah and Seth's workers weren't there today, but there would be other opportunities to meet them, she was told. That suited her fine since she had never been good with names. From what she'd been told, each of the brother's properties had at least three or more workers; some far more. Not that she was surprised – the *Broken Arrow Ranch* property was huge. Bigger than the entire township of Halliwell.

Mabel continued to sit between Clarissa and Jacob, which suited her just fine. The young girl was so sweet and affectionate. "Did you know I can ride horses?" The question came out of the blue, and for a moment Clarissa was taken unawares. "Old Nellie is my horse but she's very slow."

Seth grinned and Abigail covered a smile with her hand.

"Is that so," Jacob asked seriously. He too grinned but didn't elaborate for Clarissa's benefit. She was quite confused by the conversation.

"One day I might get a faster horse." She stared pointedly at Seth who was obviously the person holding all the strings in this situation. At least in Mabel's eyes.

"Old Nellie is perfectly fine for a five year old," Seth said sternly as he tried to force back a chuckle. "When you are older, we might look at letting you ride a little faster."

Mabel's eyes opened wide in excitement. "Really? How old? Six? I'll be six soon," she said excitedly.

"Really, Mabel," Abigail said in exasperation. "You are far too young to go faster, and you know it."

Clarissa reveled in the conversation, realizing this was what she had to look forward to one day. She glanced around at everyone assembled here and warmth flooded every part of her being. Jacob's arm slipped around her back, and she leaned into him. At least as much as she could with Mabel tucked between them.

"Do you know how much I love you," Jacob asked quietly.

His words startled her – she had no idea he felt that way, but it filled her with warmth. "I love you too," she whispered, and meant every word of it. "I love all of this too," she said, as tears threatened at the back of her eyes. She had waited for this all of her life and knew this is where she belonged – with Jacob, his brothers, and their families on *Broken Arrow Ranch*. It was a very special place indeed, and one that filled her heart with happiness.

Clarissa hooked her arm through Jacob's as they headed off for their evening walk. He couldn't speak for his wife, but he'd eaten far too much at the picnic today. Family picnics were something they tried to do regularly, because despite all of them living on the one property, they didn't often get to see each other due to work and other commitments.

The property was extensive, by far the largest in the area, and they all had their separate lives, so making the time to get together regularly was important. Family was everything to Jacob. Especially now they all had their own families. His mother would roll over in her grave if, as the oldest son, he did not ensure they all kept in touch.

It was something Jacob liked to do as he loved his brothers dearly. From her reaction today, he was certain Clarissa had enjoyed the day too, although she seemed a little tired now. "You're very quiet." He glanced down into her face and studied her closely. Something seemed different about her, but he couldn't put his finger on it.

"I'm a little tired, that's all."

He suddenly stopped walking, and she almost tripped. Jacob pulled his wife close against him. "Sorry. I didn't mean to trip you up." he told her. "Do you want to go home?"

She shook her head. "The fresh air is nice." She glanced across to where they'd picnicked earlier. "It is beautiful out here. It's so serene and captivating, I could sit and watch over the horses all day."

Jacob felt the same way, although he wasn't interested in being hands on with them, but loved to watch them. They were so graceful when they moved and were always interested in visiting with anyone who got close enough to the fences to pet them.

"It truly is. When I was a small boy, I used to come down here. I'd sit on the railing and watch the cowboys break the horses in. I even thought about becoming a cowboy myself when I got older."

She turned to stare at him. "What happened? You don't go near the horses now."

He shook his head at the memory. "I thought I was infallible, as most children do, and jumped down one day. I ran over to where Chance was breaking in a newcomer. He was a mustang, wild as they come, and I got too close too quickly and startled him. The dang thing attacked. He bit me, then reared up on his back legs." He stared down at the ground at the memory. "It took Chance forever to calm that horse back down. He was furious at me, and rightly so."

"That must have been terrifying."

"It was, and I was petrified of horses from that day onwards. I still won't go near them." He glanced down into her face. "What about you? Does anything scare you?"

She swallowed hard, then licked her lips. "There's nothing I'm truly afraid of, but I have a recurring dream that horrifies me." She swallowed again, then looked up at him. "In the dream, my brothers come here and take me back home to marry one of the suitors they chose. Stupid, I know." She turned away from him as if embarrassed.

Jacob pulled her close and cradled her head. "It will never happen. I couldn't bear to let you go."

Clarissa glanced up at him, her eyes opened wide in surprise. "Do you mean that?"

"I really do. I fell in love with you almost as soon as you arrived. At first, I thought I just felt sorry for you, but I quickly realized it was far more than that." He caressed her cheek, then cradled her face, kissing her as though there was no tomorrow.

They stood entwined for the longest time, a light breeze rustling the leaves on the trees. When Jacob looked up, the sun was beginning to set, and the sky was far more beautiful than he remembered. He reluctantly pulled away from Clarissa to show her God's work, and they stood there together taking in the wonderous canvas He had provided for them.

In that moment, Jacob understood that everything would be all right. His heart overflowed with love, and that was the most important thing at that moment in time.

The women piled into the kitchen, bringing dishes of food to share. "You didn't have to do that," Laura told Abigail as she placed the large dish of stew on the table.

"You deserve a night off," she said firmly. "Besides, there are far too many of us for you to be cooking for."

Mary strolled in not long afterwards, placing two loaves of bread in the center of the table, then handed Laura a large basket of muffins for later. "There's cold chicken too," she said quietly.

Clarissa sat in the sitting room, watching all the commotion. As much as she'd prefer to be in the kitchen, she'd been banished since it was her birthday.

It was the first time she could remember anyone fussing over her for a birthday since she was five years old. She'd been given a pony, much to Mother's disgust as she felt Clarissa was far too young. Father had arranged for one anyway. Despite the costs involved, she barely got to ride that pony. She understood now it was all about the prestige. It meant Father could boast he'd brought a pony for his daughter's fifth birthday. She was nothing but a token to him, and it cut her to her core.

"Having fun yet?" Jacob's voice over her shoulder brought her back to the present.

She turned to him and grimaced. "I've been banished. I feel like a child who has been made to stand in the corner."

His look of horror was not lost on Clarissa. It seems Laura was a far more lenient governess than the one Clarissa had bringing her up. A gentle hand came down on her shoulder. "It's not like that. Everyone loves you and wants to help celebrate your special day."

Mabel came running into the room, and Jacob's arm reached out and snatched the child up. "No running in the house, Mabel." His voice was firm, but kind. She knew Jacob could never be cruel and was the best uncle possible. She was certain he would make a wonderful father. "Can you stay with Aunt Clarissa? She's feeling a bit sad." He glanced across at her, and his eyes danced with mischief. He knew Mabel would keep her busy.

"You can't be sad on your birthday, Aunty," Mabel told her, then reached out and hugged her tightly. She placed a sloppy kiss on her cheek and sat herself on the arm of the chair with her aunt. Clarissa's heart fluttered with the affection emanating from her new-found niece. This family was special. They cared so much it made her heart hurt. How she ever survived with the Reyes clan, Clarissa would never know. Of course, she had no knowledge of what good families were really like.

Mabel covered Clarissa's hand with her own, then leaned in and whispered loudly. "Aunty made a special cake for your birthday, but it's a secret." Clarissa couldn't help but smile. Her heart was overflowing with love for these people, her family. People who loved her for who she was, and not the fact she was once an heiress.

There was suddenly a cacophony of noise behind her, and when she turned to check, Floyd, Karl, and Chance all strode through the door with Noah and Seth not far behind them. Her brothers-in-law each carried a child. In just a few months, her family had grown, and if her suspicions were correct, it would soon grow even more.

Epilogue

Almost two years later…

Clarissa stared out the window yearning to be outside. She still enjoyed the walks she and Jacob took each evening when the weather allowed. She reveled in the fresh air and the wind as it brushed past her. And she loved the feel of Jacob's hand in hers, and to simply know he was there by her side.

She leaned back into him as he wrapped his arms around her and nibbled gently on her neck. As his hands slipped down to cover her swollen belly, she shivered at his touch. It seemed to take forever, but once she knew *Broken Arrow* was where she belonged, here in her husband's arms, she was content.

All the angst Clarissa had endured before she understood she was exactly where she was meant to be had evaporated. She was surrounded by people who loved her and cherished her very being. She was resolute in her determination to never return to her blood family – the people who had ridiculed and banished her from the only home she'd ever known.

"Do you know how much I love you?" Jacob whispered the words in her ear.

His words made her smile, and warmth flooded her entire being. "At least as much as I love you." She turned in his arms and snuggled up as close as she possibly could given her condition. She glanced up into Jacob's face and her heart fluttered at the love she saw there.

There was a time when she was angry at Teddy, the family solicitor, for sending her to Jacob as his proxy bride. But she now understood the man was wise beyond his years. Not only did she need Jacob in her life, but he needed her as well. They'd saved each other.

He leaned in and kissed her lips, and a thrill went down her spine. If they lived for another eighty years, Clarissa was certain the pleasure of his touch would never leave her.

Suddenly their serenity was interrupted by the wailing of baby Barnabas. As the oldest of the family, Jacob felt it his duty to name their first born son after his father. Besides being a name that had been passed down through generations, it was a strong, prestigious name to be proud of.

She reluctantly pulled out of her husband's arms and reached down into the crib for the baby. Jacob was quickly by her side and stared down at their son as though he still couldn't believe the child existed, that he was a father. He was a wonderful father, as she knew he would be, and she couldn't wait until Barnabas was old enough for Jacob to play with.

Clarissa stared down into the angelic face of her son, his little eyes sparkling with trust for her. She wondered if she had looked at her mother's servants that way, if her Mother had ever held her this way? She pulled Barnabas close against her, letting her son hear her heartbeat. After quickly changing his wet diaper, she then turned to the comfortable chair Jacob had installed in the nursery he'd prepared for their new arrival and began to nurse their young son. His crying soon stopped, and she pondered the life she would have had if she hadn't married Jacob. She knew it would have been a life of misery, and thanked God for giving her the foresight to go to Teddy, even if he did withhold certain information from her. In his wisdom, she was certain Teddy knew exactly what he was doing and wondered if his match-making days were over.

Somehow, she thought they probably weren't.

The End

From the Author

Thank you so much for reading my book – I hope you enjoyed it.

I would greatly appreciate you leaving a review where you purchased, even if it is only a one-liner. It helps to have my books more visible!

Look out for more books in the Brides of Broken Arrow series.

About the Author

Multi-published, award-winning and bestselling author Cheryl Wright, former secretary, debt collector, account manager, writing coach, and shopping tour hostess, loves reading.

She writes both historical and contemporary western romance, as well as romantic suspense.

She lives in Melbourne, Australia, and is married with two adult children and has six grandchildren. When she's not writing, she can be found in her craft room making greeting cards.

Links:

Website: *http://www.cheryl-wright.com/*

Blog: *http://romance-authors.com/*

Facebook Reader Group:
https://www.facebook.com/groups/cherylwrightauthor/

Join My Newsletter:

https://cheryl-wright.com/newsletter/